BUNNIES AND THEIR SPORTS

BUNNIES
and Their Sports

By Nancy Carlson

PUFFIN BOOKS

Dedicated to children everywhere
who get out and exercise

PUFFIN BOOKS
Published by the Penguin Group
Viking Penguin Inc., 40 West 23rd Street, New York, New York 10010, U.S.A.
Penguin Books Ltd, 27 Wrights Lane, London W8 5TZ, England
Penguin Books Australia Ltd, Ringwood, Victoria, Australia
Penguin Books Canada Ltd, 2801 John Street, Markham, Ontario, Canada L3R 1B4
Penguin Books (N.Z.) Ltd, 182–190 Wairau Road, Auckland 10, New Zealand

Penguin Books Ltd, Registered Offices: Harmondsworth, Middlesex, England

First published in the United States of America by Viking Penguin Inc., 1987
Published in Picture Puffins, 1989
3 5 7 9 10 8 6 4 2
Copyright © Nancy Carlson, 1987
All rights reserved

LIBRARY OF CONGRESS CATALOGING IN PUBLICATION DATA
Carlson, Nancy L.
Bunnies and their sports/by Nancy Carlson. p.   cm.
Summary: Reveals bunnies involved in jogging, swimming, and exercising at the gym.
ISBN 0-14-050617-9
1. Sports—Juvenile literature. 2. Physical fitness—Juvenile literature.
[1. Rabbits—Wit and humor. 2. Physical fitness—Wit and humor.] I. Title.
[GV707.C35 1989]   796—dc 19   88–26527   CIP   AC

Printed in Japan by Dai Nippon Printing Co. Ltd.
Set in Bookman Light

Every morning when bunnies wake up from a good night's rest...

they brush their teeth, eat their breakfast,

and warm up.

Then it's time for bunnies and their sports!!!

Some bunnies like to jog…

others like to hike.

There are swimmer bunnies,

and bunnies who do swan dives.

Competitive bunnies like to play softball,

or touch football.

There are waterskiing bunnies,

and there are snow bunnies.

Sometimes many bunnies gather together

for a game of volleyball....

Brave bunnies go surfing,

or climb high mountains.

There are bunnies who go to gyms…

to lift weights,

...play basketball,

or do aerobics.

There are bunnies who roller-skate,

and bunnies who ice-skate.

Some bunnies like to exercise quietly by doing yoga,

or scuba diving deep underwater.

Some bunnies exercise outdoors, playing soccer, biking,

or playing tennis!!

Different bunnies like

different sports…

but all bunnies do sports because
they make them feel good!!!